"Reading Tatiana Ryckman's intense *I Don't Think of You (Until I Do)* was a dangerous read for a recovered romantic obsessive like me. I found myself stepping dangerously into territory from which I had believed myself weaned: unrequitedness, yearning, and the sweet hurt that accompanies the two. I was seduced back into those feelings, that familiar romantic world, by Tatiana's poetic words of want."
— Elizabeth Ellen, author of *PERSON/A*

"*I Don't Think of You (Until I Do)* makes me believe the longing and devastation of a love unfulfilled is greater than the love itself. This book bleeds that way. It feels necessary as hell, and lets me believe in art over the thing it represents. Is that possible? I don't know, but Tatiana's prose is so masterful, its tenderness and seizure is something I never want to be released from. I adore this book."
— Jon-Michael Frank, author of *How's Everything Going? Not Good*

"A voyage into the timeless whorl of when you are obsessed with someone far away. A romantic wound that keeps reinventing itself. When you can't look away from the car wreck of your own desire as you're passing it by."
— Mark Leidner, author of *Under the Sea*

First printing: September 2017

Paperback ISBN 978-1-892061-81-2

Cover art and design by Kyle Butler
Interior layout by Tyler Meese

Future Tense Books
PO Box 42416
Portland, OR 97242

futuretensebooks.com

Future Tense Books are distributed by Small Press Distribution
spdbooks.org

I Don't Think Of You

(Until I Do)

TATIANA RYCKMAN

Future Tense Books
portland, oregon

0.0

I believed it was the end.
Every time.
And it was the belief that made you a religion.

I prayed at the foot of my memories:
How we didn't see each other in the aisles of the gas
station around the corner from your apartment, where
we'd walked together once before, drunk on our new-
ness and its possibility. I'd gone in search of a bathroom
that wasn't there. You approached the counter after me
to pay for the beers we'd drink quietly at your window
in a few minutes, but I was distracted by my elemental
need and you didn't recognize me in the place where
you belonged.
Your expression when we arrived at the entrance to
your building at the same time.

Was I supposed to be farther away?
I noticed you, you said.

I had sweat my clothes see-through on the drive across
six state lines to the place where you lived, and we took
the stairs to your apartment with slow, deliberate steps.
I wanted to watch you ascend forever. I wanted to weep
at the precision of your movements. You lived as far
from me as any god I'd known, and what I would later
identify as insecurity and frustration and fear of loss

and rejection felt in that moment like reverence.

I waited in the hall as you readied a surprise. A physical manifestation of our mutual enthusiasm. But I was already holding back. I could not ignore the pain of my physical existence. I was biting my tongue and stopping myself from sacrificing the contents of my bladder to the weight of your door.
I wondered if I would ever grow used to the feeling. If I'd have the chance.

It was the most romantic moment of my whole life, and that seemed to embarrass you.

0.1

One evening while taking up space in your apartment, I took a photo of you. The sun had set and you didn't anticipate the flash in the dark room. As the air cooled, the hairs on my arms stood on end and I wished I were closer; you were only across the room but any distance greater than touching always felt impossibly far. I wondered what your image would mean when I saw it in the future, and I thought of Susan Sontag's assertion that "there is something predatory in the act of taking a picture ... it turns people into objects that can be symbolically possessed."

I didn't ask for the feeling to be mutual, only if it was.

0.2

In your presence, I rejected my aversion to the word and started to call it love. I accepted my defeat. The possibility that I cared more than you did.
But I never said so to you.
Instead, on our first warm days together, I said, *Marry me*, and laughed. And you laughed, and I died a little bit that whole beautiful day as we traveled to the top of city hall and carefully promised nothing.

But when I walked to my car, packed for my return to the place I called home but kept leaving, you said, *Let me know when you're back, and we'll think of each other*. And so my fantasy began.

0.3

Once, in middle school, I went into the city with my dad on a cultural excursion. Across the street from wherever we were—a restaurant or theater—a woman jumped out of her seat at an outdoor café. She screamed and ran, uninhibited and unencumbered despite very high heels, toward a man wearing a suit. She leapt into his arms and wrapped her legs around him. He said nothing, but he held her like that for a long time.

I had never seen anything like it before.

0.4

In your absence, I hoped that you only thought of yourself when I did, so that no one would know you like us, but this was just another opportunity to confuse me for you. Disappearing inside love was a habit they'd encouraged in my youth: "He who unites himself with the Lord is one with Him in spirit," First Corinthians read. A reminder that we are what we worship—a conveniently narrow separation between worshiping something bigger than ourselves and the best thing we can come up with. Rimbaud wrote, "I is an other."

I wondered if, like running from religion, I would always leave you in an attempt to preserve the difficulty of wanting you. I hoped so.

0.5

But it wasn't the distance that felt so insurmountable, it was the time.

Months after driving away from your front door, I drove through a town I used to visit on elementary school field trips. Winter was supposed to be over, but the landscape was a familiar non-season brown and rain dotted the windshield. Kid Rock came on the rental car radio to sing an awful song about teenage sex. He expressed a desire to "see that girl again." I suspected, though, that he didn't want to see the woman that girl had become. He wanted to lust after a version of her held hostage in his selective memory. At best, he maybe wanted to find an old photograph, something that would confirm the perfect simplicity of his idealized illusion of the past. But possibly he meant he'd settle for hooking up with her daughter. The sentiment seemed like a smear on a spectrum from blindly nostalgic to generally repulsive.

And yet, I understood. I knew we were still tethered when I found an outmoded version of me still lingering. The one that had invited myself into your apartment to watch you smoke cigarettes at your window as we both became awkward with excitement. We were tight-lipped and nervous. Our midwestern prayer: *Please like me.* The corners of your mouth twitching into a smile, you looked at me as if we were already irreversibly intertwined.

I'd still like to see you that way. And me too.

0.6

There were many things I did not say. Though it probably didn't seem like it.

In spring I went on a long walk to the nicer, farther grocery store. I saw a blackbird eating a snake and a child eating ice cream. Flowers filled the street. A cat ran into the sewer. Everything was retreating into something else. I wanted to show you everything, but you were unavailable and I couldn't imagine you would care about something I didn't want badly enough to keep to myself.

Perhaps I'd had it all backwards: Perhaps I could only think of me when you did.

When I arrived at the store, a woman sang, "you control my thoughts" over the loudspeaker.

0.7

As my flight from one faraway city to another equally remote from you prepared for takeoff, you texted to say I should stop by. It had been nearly a year since we'd walked together to buy tallboys so I would have the courage to kiss you for the first time. I'd spent our time apart hoping you'd to ask me to come and the sudden impossibility of your suggestion struck me as either uncharacteristically romantic or par for the course. It relit the thing it always seemed you were trying to extinguish.

I was on my way to a wedding where I'd pretend to think of nothing but the eternal marital bliss of a distant cousin, but I wouldn't be able to. It would be just a few degrees too cold to be comfortable in the historic church and an aunt would cry ambiguous tears of joy or lamentation. Children would look bored. I would think automatically of the opening sequence to the show *Daria*, and wish you were there, or that I weren't.

Two rows ahead of me, an older couple passed *The New York Times* and a scientific journal and the in-flight magazine back and forth across the aisle, pointing out headlines about the polar ice caps and national security and recipes that included a lot of avocado. They adjusted their glasses and read over each other's shoulders. They looked well-maintained and wore sensible shoes. They passed the crossword back and forth, each watching the other's face for acknowledgement that the clue was difficult, or a promise that they were the sole keeper of the esoteric knowledge that would solve the puzzle.

How could I not think of you?

0.8

When, after long months apart, you called yourself The Other, I realized how separate we were, more than distance.

I hadn't thought of you as The Other, only as The. As Me. So much so that I could not delineate between my image of you and the parts of you that had inserted themselves into my image of myself. But when you called yourself The Other, there was a tear in the fabric of my fantasies, and it was just one of a million final straws.

0.9

But then—
I believed so much in our endings that they were
perpetually beginning again.

1.0

This is how easy it was:

I saw a cartoon of two mice fucking and thought of you and let myself think "us."

And because a mouse on its back called out: "This feels so right!" And because this phrase so nearly echoed the things I'd repeated in my own mind while lying on my back, reimagining you filling the space I carved out of myself and how right it felt at the time that I felt it, I began to question the rightness of the feeling I was reimagining in which you were participating in absentia. Your notbeing standing in for being. And because I'd begun to doubt my own recollections and their validity, and the colors I'd applied to my memory of the shadows that compose you, I wanted to find something concrete to fill the gaps. And so I looked up lingerie on eBay and jerked off to Asians in four-dollar heart-shaped pasties. Three times. And went to sleep in the mess.

1 . 1

Everything took on the nebulous hue of an affair.
Because sometimes, while another lover prepared breakfast, I wanted to fuck you in a snowbank.

Other times, I caught a glimpse of my reflection in a window.
Startled by the image, I'd believe for a moment that I was not alone.

You moved swiftly into the spaces where you could have been if you weren't moving into other spaces that I was also suddenly interested in—the filter of a cigarette painted gold by your lungs. A steering wheel or doorknob, everything that fit under your hands. The pieces of fabric you slid your body in and out of. In and out. The painfully practical gestures of your invisible life turned erotic when I imagined them acted out over my grocery purchases, your distant movements obscuring small talk with the cashier.
The pornographic everyday of every day. Every day.

1.2

Just as every sentence and song and landscape gained meaning from its orbit around you, you changed only in relation to myself. You were the recipient of all the overwrought lyrics on the Smiths CD that had been skipping on my car stereo for years and the mood I projected on the condiments growing pillowy clouds of mold in my refrigerator, and I wondered how my life would look through your eyes and if you'd ever see it. But that didn't matter, either. Your ideas were just thoughts I presented on your behalf in the endless conversation we carried on in my mind.

But why do I say *we* when I mean *I emptied myself into the idea of you*?

Perhaps this was the source of my shame: I could no longer delineate between you and my thoughts of you, which is to say, myself.

1 . 3

At the base of a mountain, I made a list of the things I was still able to think of without you.
Each object a safe place where I could remember the world existed before you became it, but as soon as I asked the hairbrush to define itself by its notyouness, it inherited a new way of being you. The stories I imagined of your own relationship to these objects erased my memories of them. You were the things that are you and the things that are not you and the thin lines that connect all of these.

I am not a cannibal, but how else could I execute the full expression of my desire to consume you, for my cells to know you, for my body to be your body?

1.4

anvil headphones hairbrush construction cone cracked asphalt frayed shoelace athletic sunglasses glowing gate numbers at airports tall grass rusted nails cats sleeping in the sun dirt under my nails vents that blow hot air teeth left in a clean, white jaw in the woods tiny eyeball-shaped lights the plastic handle of my toothbrush cardboard boxes stacked behind grocery stores baseball caps soccer soccer moms minivans and rocks, even the ones that are almost heart-shaped that some asshole will pick up and call a heart when really it's just a fucking rock that barely even looks like Ohio.

Even that wouldn't remind me of you (until it did).

1 . 5

In an interview, Claudia Rankine said, "We're invested in [things], despite the fact that they are not good for us and place us in a non-sovereign relationship to our own lives."
I kept quoting this line while everyone on the internet rallied against the ugliness of the world.
I slotted concerns about police brutality and racism and rape and the lineage of injustice between thoughts of you.
I kept quoting this line when I rolled over in the dark cloak of my own tendency toward self-destruction.

Were you the rocks I elected to break myself against?
Are we all as helpless as we feel—when we watch the news?

You visited me at my grandfather's house on the other side of your town. That I used to think of your town as my own was the excuse I had for always coming back. We learned romance like it was new under the watchful eyes of my childhood while Fox serenaded us through the floorboards.

Is any of it connected? Is any of it not connected?

1 . 6

I hated to think the shrine of my devotion was just borrowed from the forgotten names that came before yours. You were different.
I couldn't possibly have felt this way before.

1.7

I grew restless with my inability to replace you with math or the study of foreign languages. I pretended to know the difference between anxiety and a lack of impulse control. Facebook suggested we become friends because I kept composing messages made of all the gym equipment I wanted to have sex with you on.
Did you have fantasies? I did.
I'd ask you to marry me and you'd say no and we would never talk again and just feel a little unhappy for the rest of our lives but would never be able to know how that feeling differed from the alternatives.

When I said forever, did you think *together* or *not together*?

1.8

As I undressed for bed in my cold apartment, your smell came out of my clothes and what struck me was not that you could linger for months on my skin but that the smell was at once unfamiliar and unmistakable. Your body or detergent or maybe the smell of the room you were born in. But as soon as I tried to grasp it, it slipped away, as if it had never been there at all.

The toes of my shoes nudge the doorframe and my breath condenses on thick white paint. I lick the ridges in the wood, masked by a layer of white for each tenant who has lived here before me. If I'm careful, I'll see archaic opulence through the window of my closed eyes. The view from your sheets was pink with daylight and the domed roofs of banks, and I memorized dust motes piercing the sun before it could hit us. The breath that gathers between my face and the wall could be yours if I don't shake the snow globe of my memory and erase you riding elevators to views of the Great Lakes we've each lived on and off, where we could still meet and shiver at the top of a mound of government paperwork.

You didn't ask me to stay, but maybe it's not too late for that.

1.9

The flight from my city to yours took exactly one-eighth the time required to drive the same distance.

I considered the magic of being catapulted through space as I was violently shaken to sleep. When the window became impossibly dark, I placed four peanuts at a time on my tongue and sucked away the salt. I swallowed.
I repeated *Flesh of my flesh*.
Again.

2.0

I found myself entering *I am very depressed* into Google
so I would feel less alone.

2.1

Words like *hungry* and *empty* and *gutted* and *open* seemed to vary in texture, but not meaning.
I lost my appetite.
I'd read about this in magazines and poems. But starving myself from missing you seemed unsustainable.
Everything did.

2.2

Because all of my grand gestures were neurons train-hopping on thoughts of you, you couldn't see them from the other side of my skull or the country. Every thought was another plan to prove my devotion that you didn't respond to.

And I didn't blame you because no one is a mind reader, I hear.

And we all get busy.

And you got very busy.

When I didn't hear from you for days, I began to imagine, in torturous detail, that busy meant someone else was moving you from one all-consuming task to the next. From the bed we'd shared to the floor I hadn't had a chance to claim with my body on yours. From the specific taste of their sweat to the art they inspired you to make. Every truncated message you sent was an example of your infatuation with the person I'd imagined for the explicit purpose of seducing you away from me.

Soon, between the flights I took in my mind to your room and the ways I'd hold you in my mouth and the monument you'd once built to our hours together in your living room, this someone else would occasionally step out of my own fantasies of you to remind me how far away I really was.

2.3

I once knew a woman whose daughter had died very young and had been gone a long time. The woman spoke constantly of her child's wisdom and brave spirit. One day I met the woman's son. I was shocked by his existence, but I understood.
You were my dead daughter—there was no room in my sorrow for anyone else. Least of all the people who were really there.

But during long periods of silence, I would convince myself that nothing had transpired between us. That my willingness to undo my life at your feet was as ordinary as lust.

But then you might write, *Hey*.
And I would reply that I'd spread myself out thinking of you, already eight times that day, a loop of you pressing me against your desk conflated with two Danish women writhing on the floor of a rowboat still playing in my mind.
And you wouldn't say anything at all.

2.4

Months after using my camera, I developed a roll of film and found you on it. I thought of Sontag writing, "The sense of the unattainable that can be evoked by photographs feeds directly into the erotic feelings of those for whom desirability is increased by distance." I felt obvious and became embarrassed.

But when I thought you were far enough away, and that I wasn't pining or wistful, I examined your photo with a scientific closeness. I discovered your face was a punishment.

Because even if I could add this replica of you to the altar where I prayed for your nearness, I'd been warned against graven images, their ability to divert attention from the true object of worship, and I couldn't allow anything to come between me and my fidelity. Not even you.

2.5

I couldn't help but notice that you were probably not in love.
Not with me, anyway. Which is not to say I would admit that I was. Not at that distance, anyway.

But from my backyard, I noticed both the lack of you and the prevalence of mosquitoes and it felt like being alone at a party. Like watching my phone as if I had friends on the way. But I was just pretending to nature that you'd show up.

A friend received a note from their boss that read, *I'm waiting to see something really great from you.*
I wondered if this was what you'd been trying to tell me all along.

2 . 6

I attempted self-improvement. I collected thick books by my bed and stared at their pages hoping to replace the memory of the pale skin of your forearms with political unrest. So distracted was I by my own suffering in the world I'd invented, where you were riding on the shoulders of love and success and an eternal, boring happiness, that it was not you who disappeared from my fantasies, but I.
I told myself that the rotating cast of people I dreamed in my place were everything you'd ever wanted.

One night, a coworker fell in love with me when we finished selling noodles. *I'll replace your partner*, they offered, *if you replace mine*. But I'd decided independently that if anyone were going to be replaced, it was probably me.

2.7

How did it happen, then, that I was in your car? Even as we were propelled across frozen northern states at seventy miles an hour, I struggled to believe it.

I must have asked for a favor as a means of throwing myself back into your life. A ride from somewhere out of your way to a place we would both be headed. And you agreed for reasons I still don't understand.
I wondered if I could take solace in the fact that I wasn't torturing myself alone.
You stood behind me, and with your hand over mine, showed me just how to bring down the whip.

When we arrived, you said, *Can we lie down for a moment?*

We were in the same bed my mind had been caught in for months. The blankets were thicker and the click of the radiator played in the background, but your shirts were still hanging behind us and Sonic Youth CDs were still piled by our heads. It was code for *Will it go better this time?* and I felt the deceptive allure of normalcy.

2.8

At the holiday party the next night, I was just waiting for your friends to leave. The entire city's enthusiasm kept coming between us. We pressed our lips together as the ball descended above us, but I didn't care that the year was dying; I didn't worry that I was leaving anything behind.

2.9

One of us always had to be somewhere and the other had to leave, and there was no way to fold geography into itself. The atlas warping with rain and coffee in my backseat could not bring our cities any closer to one another, and as we slept together my last night in your town, you became more real as I began to fade into wherever it was I was going next.

At the airport, I promised to leave myself there, to be back, to stay longer next time, to stay.
But when I returned to what we kept calling real life, you retreated behind the mask of memory and though I watched for you in the shitty glow of my computer screen, nothing happened.
Again.

3.0

For a while I thought my memories were enough to stand in for you, but even my imagination had limits. Like how every time I touched myself, you were in the same shadow.

I replayed the same loop of three women inserting produce into each other on a kitchen table and our feet caught in the same blankets.
We kept saying the same things: *Fuck*, and *Oh, God*, and *Come for me*.
Sweat pooled in the same hidden places between us and behind my knees.

If I projected you in my mind through a new summer, would you notice? And I guessed not. I guess that's how everything stayed exactly the same.

3 . 1

Our special nothing took more strategy than seemed reasonable and I lost patience.

When did my infatuation become pragmatic? When you finally asked why I wasn't there, it seemed after the fact. Beside the point.

I was already beside myself. Standing idly nearby, watching nothing unfold between us.

I remembered:

You were tattooing my foot with crustaceans and I was at the foot of your bed and you were looking away. It is possible that you dog-eared the place where I left myself. That what I longed for when I longed for you was to be alone.

3.2

I was so prepared for our failure that I couldn't bring myself to add you to the endless whir of social media; I couldn't bear a privileged glimpse into your life without me. I didn't want all my suspicions confirmed. When you eventually pointed out that I was being hypocritical, I couldn't argue, but it still seemed like I was the only one who could get hurt.

3.3

You were the ocean or a rabbit hole.
—Or one of those cardboard structures on the outskirts
of midsized towns, renting for $300 a week. A steal for
someone who's got nowhere else to go.

3.4

I remembered that, once, after returning to your town, I hoped for hours that you would appear and you did. We'd only met once before, but the ease with which we'd found ourselves in your apartment was disorienting and promising and distracted me for weeks as I drove to other faraway cities making new mistakes colored by my fresh interest in you.

When I saw you again, the glory of your arms in a T-shirt brought to mind all the walls we hadn't pressed each other against. I was sick with the feeling that there was nothing about you I couldn't fall in love with.

You invited me in and asked, *Can we lie down for a moment?* and when I remembered that, I worried that we would see each other again. Or that we wouldn't.

3.5

My feeling for you was like the feeling everyone has a
few weeks after a global tragedy.
The disconnect between the grocery store and war ren-
dering everything meaningless. What is senseless about
killing when meat is on sale?
Ukraine is writing love letters to Russia. Terrorism is a
birthday party, and planes nap peacefully at the bottom
of the sea.
Even the ticker tape of my fantasies grew disenchanted.

Sometimes I longed for my longing, even knowing
it wouldn't fix anything except how much I missed
missing.
Sometimes I didn't, though.
Sometimes I just forgot to think about you.

3.6

At some point, demarcated by the same distance that had existed between us for an indeterminate amount of time, I started seeing someone new.

I tried to reinvest my feelings for you in them. As if all I needed was a vessel to carry the weight of my desire. This new person could not tell the difference, but when they said they loved me, I questioned the ethics of my behavior.

To compensate, I devoted myself to them completely.

3.7

I became very tired.

3 . 8

In the bathroom at my office job, I pretended I was inside your skin and I made your face into the mirror, the face I had been carrying in me for months. On me, it was unbecoming and I knew it would never win your affection the way it had won mine.

I remembered:
Your pants had fit both of us perfectly, but I wondered which of the three of us, you and me and the pants, fit best in which of the others and so on. For a terrible moment, the Venn diagram of our mutual existence seemed to rely entirely on a pair of Levi's.

3.9

On the drive to buy out-of-season spinach, a Tina Turner song came on the radio. Everywhere I was was just another place you weren't. The beige concrete of the South slipped by my window at a speed above the posted limit, and my skin clung to the car seat. I was worrying over definitions, whether I had perhaps misunderstood love all along.

But Turner asked what love had to do with it, and I remembered that there was nothing remarkable about heartbreak.

4.0

But there was no more escaping you than the inevitable
return of summer.

When I saw you again, it was in the same place as always and exactly as I had feared or hoped.
You walked into the room you'd walked into the year
before, and we sat close pretending we ever sit close, and
we went to dinner with mutual friends pretending we
ever go to dinner with mutual friends, and our friends
tried to pretend I would not be going home with you
until the lie was more awkward than the reality.

4.1

You asked, *Can we lie down for a moment?* And so little
had changed, I suspected that our former selves, too,
were tucked somewhere in the walls. I bit my tongue.
I did not run through the apartment announcing my
love for the illusion that this thing could endure. I did
not jump into your arms; I did not wrap myself around
you. Instead, we fell asleep as we discussed which bar to
meet our friends at later.

But we never made it, to no one's surprise.

4.2

We woke while it was still dark and had sex as the sun came up and you said, *That's nice*, and I didn't know which part you were talking about and I didn't ask. A sheet hung in the window to block the sun but it also recreated the scene I'd played in my mind of the sun in your window reflecting off a thin shower of dust the year before and I was forced to confront the two figments of my imagination, or memories, or versions of us, and what they might mean. I was waiting for everything to present itself as a significant plot point from which I could proceed with confidence.

I wondered if we'd pretend better this time.

4.3

We made it through the weekend with calm excitement. We were saving some for later, making plans. The thing we'd stopped saying aloud was, *How long can this really last?*

In bed, you put your hands together in a way that made me think *Here Is the Church, Here Is the Steeple,* but you meant that we should put our heads between each other's legs and it was like a code in a dream that only the dreamer understands, and I was passing into wakefulness.

I remember most clearly the queasy, persistent optimism.

4.4

A mutual friend made it clear that no matter whose heart was broken, they'd take your side.

4.5

I was still states away but closer than ever and struggling with not being particularly interested in anything, which was imbued with the painful hopefulness that at any moment I could become interested in everything. It wasn't that you were dead to me, but that I was.

I ate fistfulls of crackers without tasting them, just scraping the salt against my tongue.

I was confronted with the problem of getting what I wanted. The year of longing for the city of you I'd built in my mind was replaced by your nearness.
Which only made your absence more pronounced.

4.6

Your absence became you. Which is to say it cast you in a flattering light, and then you were more the light and less you, and when you could find a moment to call, we again revisited the impossibility of everything.

The distance between us grew heavier in light of how easy we had thought it would be. The belief that we were worth the five-hour drive was fading.

Maybe this was confusing because I was not angry. Maybe we'd said *There's no way it can work* enough times that it was true, and so either you would call back or you wouldn't. Either you would send indelicate photographs or I would imagine them based on educated guessing. Is that the same thing as a hypothesis? Can one hold two hypotheses at the same time? I was guessing that the outcome would be equal in any direction. You would be there or you would not, and that was one thing I could trust.

4.7

When you said you'd come to visit, I considered suggesting sex moves I'd learned from literature, like ascending to heaven and keeping all my kings in the back row. I thought it could be a secret language only we would speak, but then I thought you might not get it, like when I asked if you were seeing someone else and you thought I meant I hoped you would so I could too, and it seemed like maybe we'd never spoken the same language, not even on the most elementary level.

4.8

I suffered from a belief in the hierarchy of distance. That closer was closer no matter how inconvenient. I had faith that the faraway, real you could be animated by the you I told everything to in my mind, that you were there no matter where you were. A childhood friend from church once told me, *That's how I feel about God*.

But you said five hundred miles may as well be five thousand; not there was simply not there. And I heard, *Out of sight out of mind*.

I reminded myself there was no us, just our individual memories of what that hour-long phone call meant while I waited out a layover in Chicago and you followed the Great Lakes from one depressed city to another.

4.9

We were constantly looking for some excuse to drive very far out of our way and into each other's, or not to. I admitted a nervousness to myself: Maybe we were getting to know each other too well to like each other.

5 . 0

During a trip to Mexico, a friend of mine made a painting of a gate every day. The same gate, over and over. As an act of solidarity, or curiosity, or most likely a creative jealousy, I said that I would draw the same thing every day as well. She warned that the gate had become boring; she wished she had picked something more interesting. So she added things behind the gate. I wondered about the fake things behind her imitation of a real gate and chose to draw the bathrobe of an old man whom I had barely known, but whose house I was sleeping in for the summer.

Is it incorrect to call him old when he is dead?

This would have nothing to do with you, except that as I failed to accurately render the bathrobe, which was complicated with folds and paisleys, I imagined you instructing me as you once had, as I drew the side of your head and placed your ear much too low.

5 . 1

The thing we were calling *inevitable* turned out to be debilitating sadness.

Alone in bed I'd say, *I'm dying*, over and over again. But nothing happened. My cells regenerated at the same rate. I refreshed my empty email inbox. I was dying while making breakfast and that turned into dying while washing dishes which turned into dying in the shower and then dying in the bed again and then later, over a glass of juice. I was dying on the floor. I was dying while listening to sad music on headphones. I was dying while reading the missed connections on Craigslist. I was dying while watching videos of sleepy kittens on YouTube. I was dying while watching two women taste each other on a different website with a similar name. I was dying while making popcorn for dinner and sending smiley face text messages to friends and Liking things on Facebook. I was dying while looking at the ceiling and then the wall and back at the ceiling again. I was dying and wishing I would just die.

Anne Carson wrote that she had felt so bad the year after the end of a relationship, she had thought she could die. She wrote, "This is not uncommon." and even if we hadn't said that we were through, I still related to her observation, that "the hardest part about losing a lover / is / to watch the year repeat its days."

5 . 2

I got a new computer and took the opportunity to get rid of files I hadn't looked at in years and saw no future use for. I went through old photos and watched fifteen years of myself falling in love with someone new and then I watched them disappear. Over and over. I couldn't be sure which part of the process we were in. Then I wondered about my own permanence in your mind or hard drive.

I wondered if I would ever reappear in your life in the accident of a long-unopened file. Would I make the transfer to a new device? Did I belong in the future?

5 . 3

I tried to write you a love letter in the absence of a love letter. It read: *Look, there are many famous songs about this; certainly you must know at least one or two.* It was embarrassing and unashamed and too late.

I was getting restless and had to coach myself on appropriate behavior. I reminded myself not to copy and paste all your old messages into a new message to prove how you feel to yourself. I would not call just to see how you're doing, just to see what's going on.

In contrast to my memory, summer seemed to extend infinitely ahead of us. There would be so many bathrobes. And so little of you.

5 . 4

When I wept while reading Wikipedia I thought, this is a new low.
I read about Dorothy Tennov's study of limerence and was embarrassed by my predictability and the probability that the presence of my love was dependent on the absence of yours, and finally I wasn't crying for your invisibility but for the emptiness I had named after you. I wrote the researcher following in Tennov's footsteps and offered myself up as a subject. I'd learned not to expect anything in return, and they never responded.

I went on a walk and read a book and ate dinner with friends and eventually I felt a variation on better.

And then you called.

5 . 5

You said you were coming to visit and I immediately reorganized my worldview to allow for optimism. I hid the things I knew you liked. A shirt you'd complimented or a book I'd lent you. I was setting my best aside, as if it would be wasted on anyone else. The things I cared for most waited for you to validate them with your acknowledgment.

5 . 6

After weeks apart, I realized we would be having sex the following day, at least probably, and I touched myself and wondered if the reality of you would kill the you I'd been sleeping with in my mind. I watched one woman accidentally walk in on her friend masturbating and then shyly join in and I thought maybe my hands were not getting the pleasure they deserved. I instructed my body to give more. I told my hands to imagine I was you. It was like that thing kids try in high school where they make their hand numb so it feels like being touched by a stranger, but in reverse. I wanted to numb my body so my hands wouldn't know who they touched. I wanted to be with someone who wasn't me and I wanted to be them at the same time, and you were already a familiar stand-in.

I was surprised to find even my version of you was not what it once was. The fantasy had been obscured by a jungle of quotidian motion: Your turned head faded when I watched my memory too closely, your lips disappearing from my wrist just when I thought I had felt them.

5 . 7

A song played in the grocery store while I weighed bulk goods. It said, "I'm scared to be lonely," over and over again. I didn't want to identify with that sentiment. If anything, I was scared to be scared to be lonely. But I also didn't want to be alone with myself, and so I worried that you wouldn't either.

Later that evening, I learned that the mole I'd been watching grow into cancer on my arm had been a blister all along.
The poison ivy grew up my arms.
That this was not attractive was the excuse I made for why I was relieved that you would probably never really show up.

5.8

While waiting for you, I became bored for the first time.

5 . 9

You were on your way and I was sitting very still.
I was notdrawing the bathrobe.

You were going to arrive after dinner because distance,
because traffic. But there were more pressing concerns—the poison ivy had spread. My fingers looked
boiled. I worried over where the rash would appear
next.
The itch was retreating into something bearable, but
still unpleasant. Even with an injection at the ER, the
creams, and the pills, the situation was slow to improve.
Saying *ER* was how I found myself insinuating that my
pain had credibility.
It was the way I could say *Please care*. To say *Look, I'm
serious*.

Your arrival felt so small compared to what it was up
against that I struggled to register the significance of
your physical presence, even if it's what I kept saying
I wanted.

6.0

When you came in, I didn't touch you as much as I wanted to. There was company and the recurring lack of confidence I faced each time I faced you, and this was made worse by the weeping blisters that covered my hands. I could not shake the feeling that all my ugliness had finally surfaced.

But I longed to have our mutual existence witnessed publicly. To be obvious and uncareful.

6 . 1

When I re-see your feet between mine, the way they flexed as you tried to get closer our first night together after five unbearably long weeks, I am too distracted by the differences between our toes to think about the difficulties that made everything impossible.

I hadn't thought to worry that you'd see through my devotion and realize how uninteresting I am. I hadn't thought to worry that my devotion was thin enough to see through.

6.2

At the local fair, you and I and an ex and an old crush and a mutual friend all threw baseballs at milk jugs that never turned. It seemed like a bad joke: How many failed relationships does it take to win a stuffed animal? We ate donuts and looked at rabbits in cages.

I finally remembered that we were in my hometown when my junior prom date walked by with their many children. Where were you when they eyed me suspiciously over their dripping ice cream cones?

6.3

When you got up from the bed, you faced the window and your back was to me and you looked so much older than you had moments before. You were a silhouette against the wilderness I'd been living in.

I stayed in bed and continued to touch myself while you paced the room, already half gone. The fading light on the yellow walls and bookshelves reminded me of the many days I'd been alone. You pulled your shirt on like you were leaving. Maybe just to the next room, but it had the crushing weight of an ending.

I pressed myself back into the pillows and wished I could believe that it could be over so easily. That I could just get up and reinvest myself in my future rather than ours.

Instead I came while imagining five women fucking on a tarp, and then went to pick at cookies that had gone stale in the August humidity while you worked in the next room.

6.4

Even as you slept beside me, you were abstract.
Which is to say that I still didn't know how much I
didn't know you, so that each time I turned to study
your dark outline, you became less my imagination
and more something else, the real you, and I wondered
if I was equipped to know that person or to learn who
you were outside of myself.

That night I had a dream about someone I used to wonder if I loved, and it left a gloss over the day. I wondered
if I'd be able to see you through their ghost.
Perhaps their shadow owned so much of my mind because they never stuck around long enough to be made
real and regrettable and undesirable, as they surely
would have become in time.
It's what you call The One Who Got Away.
I always wanted you to be able to get away; I just didn't
want you to go.

6.5

We were so good at being apart that even when I was on top of you, your thumb pressing between my lips while your fingers cradled my jaw, I didn't know if I could touch you. If you'd say no, or when you'd vanish. I was trying to replace you with the image of you I'd sacrificed my longing to all year. I was distracted by the inevitability of your departure. I was distracted by the group dynamic. I was distracted by breakfast and the dog and you. Was I falling out of love or into it? Was this just what it felt like to be in the same place?

Sometimes I missed you most when you were close.

6.6

You yelled from your car as you pulled away, and I was wearing the bathrobe and I wondered if it was true, what you said. I wondered if I was a dream, some residue of reality. If I was that hard to believe in, or something you'd wake up from, or if it was just a romantic thing to yell from a car window. I had been thinking about the dream of my old lover, and after you left I read about dreams while bread baked in the oven. The dog was there.

Hélène Cixous wrote, "We are not having the dream, the dream has us."

It was domestic and common and it seemed like you were missing out, or like I was missing you, so I opened the paper packaging around your leftover carnival food and ate all the pieces you'd marked with your teeth.

6.7

The dream of my old lover faded, and over the days of steadily decreasing communication, so did you. I found that I was not a void in your absence. I remembered that just because you weren't there, didn't mean I was alone. Morrissey sang, "I don't dream about anyone except myself."

But then you started to make promises.
Two visits before the summer's end. A motel room.
My excitement was kept in check by the fear that plans are the foundation of disappointment. Would you really come back?
Would you?

6.8

I wanted to believe you would return and I followed
the pipe dream of your possible visit as far as it would
take me.

I said to a version of you I kept in my mind:
Let's assume you do come. Let's assume we find a
Motel 6 in a suburb I've never been to. A place where
I can't show you that museum I texted you from when
I was feeling mean about all the art. Let's assume we
have a six-pack and a limited number of TV channels
and the blankets are itchy and the windows don't open.
Let's assume these are our surroundings and nothing
is walking distance; that is, we can see things from the
second-story railing that wraps around the motel, but
we cannot walk to the places we see because they are
on the other side of a highway. We could drive but we
already have the six-pack, and we are unmotivated. So
we turn back to the room. You smoke a cigarette in
the doorway. I am jealous of the cigarette and want to
be in your mouth, and then maybe I will be, and then
maybe you will have my hair in your fist and I will be
thinking that I should not be thinking about how I am
always being pulled toward you, I should be thinking
about the fist that is pulling me. I should be turned on
by the four hairs you missed while shaving, but I will
be distracted by them. Then we will switch places and
I will come and we will fall asleep and then it will be
morning, and we will have to leave.

6.9

Or, let's assume you wouldn't come.
It'd just be the same shit.

7.0

I gave up drawing the bathrobe and I didn't feel guilty.

Until I did.

7 . 1

I tried not to think about you.

And then I was writing to ask what was going on, which I'd avoided for weeks. And you didn't seem to know what I meant—*What is going on?* And I tried, unsuccessfully, to say it meant nothing. Although nothing might be anything I said, desperately, at any moment.

The Violent Femmes sang, "How can I explain personal pain?"

7 . 2

The internet reminded me that everything was happening all the time. All the friends I wasn't seeing were enjoying each other's company without me. Everyone I knew seemed to be developing a mutual infatuation with podcasts about murder and acknowledging their privilege. There were parties and vacations and marriages and the bland, continuous impression that I was missing something.

Which is to say anything could have happened at any time.

Which is why I wrote to say *What is going on?* Because I believed that everything was always happening without me.

You, for example.

7.3

I arranged pillows on the bed in your general size and shape and leaned into them through long, hot afternoons while scolding myself for not being more productive.

In a fit of ennui, I made myself draw a bathrobe for you. I obscured the robe behind the ladder-back of a chair and suddenly understood my friend's impulse to imagine something new behind her gate.

I had already been convinced that if I thought about you while I drew the robes I would do a better job. Another way of saying this is that I believed that if I had sex with talented and interesting people, I would be more talented and interesting. There are formulas that corroborate this bad logic, which makes it no more accurate.

7.4

I had promised to draw every day because I thought it would make me more focused and creative, but my ambitions spiraled far beyond my capabilities. I began to hope the exercise would make me more diligent and a better person. I would discover a hidden natural skill. People would be impressed. I would make friends and develop patience and make money and would never experience failure again. I wanted to be better—not just than I had been, but better than everyone else. At least to you.

It was a lot of pressure for a dead man's bathrobe.

And us.

When I told my friend, who was no longer in Mexico and had herself given up on gates, about my defeat she said, *I mean, it's an endeavor that was always doomed to fail. No one is ever going to capture life as it was. We all decided to try something impossible.*

7.5

The next time we talked, we were practical. We started asking if we had extra time to throw at the impossibility of a relationship neither of us were willing to give anything up for.

One month later, I would sit on your bed in a familiar crushing silence and you would look away. You would call this *Modern Romance*. It had not occurred to me that, all over the world, other people were doing this same terrible dance. I thought about the lost global productivity that would result from so much agony. About the gross domestic product and efficiency and waste motion. This was the way I learned not to think about you.

7.6

You did not come back and summer ended.

7.7

I pulled the detritus of the summer into neat piles and hid it under the things I'd need. I'd spent months listening to romantic songs and had compiled lists of lines I wished I'd written to you. I fought calling to tell you everything and had the distinct impression that there was nothing I could say that wouldn't be turned into something much worse. My most heartfelt notes read like a dissertation. I'd researched the topic; I had evidence to present.

But it was never the right time.

7.8

I listened to songs about clean breaks and being better off and burning bridges, but the relief I was looking for didn't come. The obvious best choice was still obscured by remembering a long summer afternoon of accomplishing nothing together and the feeling that that could have lasted forever.

I packed my whole life into the trunk of my car so it looked like I had never been there at all. I put the bathrobe in the dresser and gathered a few books I wanted to show you when I passed through your town, which had once been my family's town, until even my association to myself was eclipsed by you.

I did an excellent job of disappearing.
As I tend to do.

7.9

I dropped a friend off at the airport on my way out of town.

While drunk one night, we had read each other's tarot. I read the cards to mean that one should strive for contentment in their love life, even if that means learning to love being alone.

Then it was my turn.

8 . 0

As I began the long drive, I supposed that I should take on a cheerfulness.

So I referenced every view I'd had of the side of your face as I sat on your bed nervous and high on my insecurity, and the times I pretended I wasn't looking you up on the internet because I missed you and all the times I came and your closed eyes as you came and the way you shape-shifted in my window the last time I'd seen you and your disembodied arm waving goodbye as you yelled from your car and how maybe everything hadn't been ruined, even if I felt ruined by it, and I remembered that this was not my dream but that I belonged to it, and that line about science. That an anecdote does not make evidence. That my feelings of self-doubt and loathing may not reflect yours, and just like that, you were made new.
Which is to say I was feeling very hopeful.

8 . 1

I made the drive in three-quarters the time predicted.
I stopped at a mutual friend's house and we talked
about work. Your name was on a flier by the door.
I had forgotten the thrill of seeing your name in the
wild, but there they were, your name and my over-
flowing desire. The words *last ditch effort* come to mind
when I remember this scene.

I projected us two hours into the future, across the city
and your bed and another cycle of whatever we'd been
doing.

8.2

But then I got caught up in the conversation.
And left late and had to get gas and you'd fallen asleep
waiting, so when I finally showed up you were smoking in the doorway and neither of us showed our excitement, if there was any left by that point, and we walked
up the steps to your apartment with only the keys on
your belt echoing in the stairwell.

We fell asleep almost immediately.
There was once a time when I was flattered by sleep,
and fell into it like a compliment. *See*, I'd say with my
narcolepsy, *this is how much we trust each other*.
But we were just tired.

8.3

The next day, I took my grandfather to get his hair cut and bought a watermelon.

While I waited around the strip mall, you and I made plans for dinner via text. You wrote, *It's a date*.
I read it over and over.

I wondered if anything we'd done in the previous year had been a date, or if this was the first, and I eyed my excitement suspiciously.

8 . 4

As we walked to a bar after dinner, I said I wanted you in a dark alley. You said you did not want to be had in a dark alley. And while I didn't blame you on a practical level, I was sad that you didn't want to want to be had in a dark alley. Not (even) by me.

When I asked if you imagined windows from the inside or outside, you didn't have an answer. And I had to convince myself that that didn't mean anything. I didn't have an answer, either.

And while neither of us could put a finger on why, the evening got worse from there.

8.5

At some point, it felt like it was always that way.
Like we had worked so hard to not mean the things
we were always stopping ourselves from saying that we
never knew what anything meant.

When we got back, you sat deliberately at a distance
while I hated myself at the edge of your bed.
If I'd asked, would you have been able to remember
why I was there?
Would I?

Ivan Klíma wrote, "We often believe that we are tied
to someone by love, and meanwhile we're only tied to
them by hate, which we prefer to loneliness."

I remembered: You were the pleasantly suffocating
blanket of hot air in my closed-up car in a southern
parking lot. I climbed into the driver's seat and you texted to say *Somewhere in a parallel universe there is a cabin
off the shore of Nova Scotia with us in it, living happily.*

8.6

When I think of all the ways I'd hoped you would choke me, I wonder: What is this desire to be punished by the people we love? Then I remember it's why people need God and parents and anyone else at all. That pain is how we know where we end and something else begins. But the pain seemed to come from inside me, as if you were peeling away, and by the time I learned the boundary between us, it had turned into something else.

8.7

I asked, *What is the best case scenario?*
And you said, *To live alone in the woods*.
I said, *That makes this easy.* That wasn't what you'd meant, you said.

You had never seemed so exasperated. I had never felt like such a chore.
And I kept holding this summer up against the one before it, wondering what had happened.

We were just close enough to be at loose ends.
You smelled of nothing.
Against all advice, we went to bed angry and managed to maintain an unseasonably cool sliver of space between us all night. I thought of the admonishment I'd heard so often in adolescence: *Leave enough room for Jesus.*

8.8

In the morning, I sipped at your coffee and we agreed. Things were no less fucked, but we were comfortable with that. It had always been this way. Nothing had changed because of one bad night, not really.

There was comfort in the resignation.
Maybe that was the problem.

8.9

But it was the first time I had questioned what right I had to my wealth of desire. The first time it occurred to me that my fantasies might not be anything to strive for. That you might not be a fantasy at all; you might just be someone who lived very far away.

9.0

And that's how it happened that I read a book and wondered what you'd think before I created a thought on your behalf.

I wondered, What is precious about wanting?

I remembered a short film a friend had burned to a disc for me in college. At the edge of a mountain or Italian scenic overlook, or likely in front of a sheet painted to look like the edge of a mountain, a blonde woman bent over a low stone wall. Another woman lost her arm deep inside the blonde while another licked contentedly at the blonde's exposed asshole. In my recollection, there is another woman, a fourth, who fondles the blonde's breasts and coaches her to come, or to come now, or to come for her. She chants encouraging phrases between performative moans of pleasure.

But there's no way to verify any of this now. I've lost the disc, and I'm not even sure all those people I imagine ever existed.

9.1

The cartoon of two mice fucking just became something sad my friend had drawn. Because while one mouse called out "This feels so right," the other mouse seemed surprised by the pronouncement, uneasy under the weight of such emotion.

9 . 2

I stopped believing there was inherent magic in things outside my control.
The news playing from my grandfather's television was just something turned up too loud.
The world was just the place where we kept all of our problems.
The books I'd elected to speak on my behalf became books you just hadn't returned yet.
The pop songs I'd attributed to you broke everyone else's heart, too.

That was the point.

9.3

And on the other side of town, when my grandfather said goodbye to a woman who could no longer remember herself, the last person left from his real life, I was surprised to find that I did not reassign their sadness to you or their separation to us. How lonely, I thought instead, to be the last thing left no one remembers.

Suddenly it seemed that everyone was counting down to some inevitable end.

9.4

So I readied myself for the inevitable.

9.5

But when I parked around the corner from your building on my last evening in town, and walked the familiar sidewalk back to the doorway where you stood smoking in the fading sunshine as everyone else in the world left their day job, the whole city distracted with the final days of summer, the thing that happened was not an ending.

The foolish lurch in my chest was not an ending.
Your expression was not an ending.

9.6

You said, *Can we lie down for a moment?*

9.7

I talked quickly about things that didn't matter on our way to meet friends for dinner.
Before the food arrived, I found that I could not remember if we were pretending we were together, or pretending we were not together.

I had to fight the temptation to project myself onto every surface of your life.
You squeezed my knee under the table as I smiled idiotically into my pasta.

We went to an event where everyone knew you.
We held hands in front of them.
We kissed quickly in dark corners and empty stairwells.
We ate phallic rainbow candy and looked for a place to undress each other.

Every empty room we found filled the moment we came close and it was getting late, so we left with the same giddiness we'd buried under distance and caution all year. It came up uncontrollably like vomit—both terrifying and promising relief.

9.8

In that final dark, it was suddenly easy to pretend it was the previous summer, as if our want was the season we'd been waiting for.

But I'd learned to fear giving you everything and held a portion of tenderness back for myself.
With your fingers in my mouth, I realized that this could be the last time we'd be together for the year. Or forever.

It seemed like the only way to have what we wanted was to be certain it would end.

9.9

In the morning, we circled the fountain in front of city hall. The air was cool and the grey-pink light bounced off of windows of nearby offices. The streets were empty and I threaded my fingers through yours.
A homeless man slept below a lion.
The building was closed for the weekend and in place of climbing to the patterned rim of its tower to look over the lake, we looked up at its decorative façade.
I bit my tongue, but you said, *We've come full circle*.

10.0

In the doorway to your apartment, we struggled to loosen our grip on one another. My face was buried in your neck; my loaded car waited at the curb. The rest of the world was a backdrop to my impending departure and a sad nothing echoed in the long stairwell spiraling above us. Everything seemed far away and pointless. Everything but you.

When I finally let go, you said, *We can still talk*, and I lied: *That's right. No one is dying.*

But I knew better. It happens all the time.

Acknowledgments:

I am grateful to the journals that published portions of this book: *Hobart*, *Muse/A*, *NumeroCinq*, and *Cosmonauts Avenue*. Many thanks also to Kevin Sampsell and Bianca Flores at Future Tense for taking this project on, and for their thoughtful edits and insights. Finally, I have endless appreciation for Kyle William Butler's brilliant cover art, Emily Roberts' meticulous copy editing, the careful reading my friends and peers gave to early drafts of this book, and Jordan Shiveley's drawing of two mice fucking, which inspired this obsessive manuscript.

Tatiana Ryckman was born in Cleveland, Ohio. She is also the author of two chapbooks of short prose, *Twenty-Something* and *VHS and Why It's Hard to Live*. Tatiana's work has appeared on *Tin House's The Open Bar*, *Hobart*, *Barrelhouse*, *No Tokens*, *The Establishment*, *Corium Magazine*, *The Collapsar*, *Fields Magazine*, *Barely South Review*, *DIAGRAM*, *The Nervous Breakdown*, *Heavy Feather Review*, and *Flavorwire*, among other publications. Tatiana has been an artist in residence at Yaddo and Arthub, and she is the editor of Awst Press and Assistant Editor at sunnyoutside press.

More info at tatianaryckman.com.